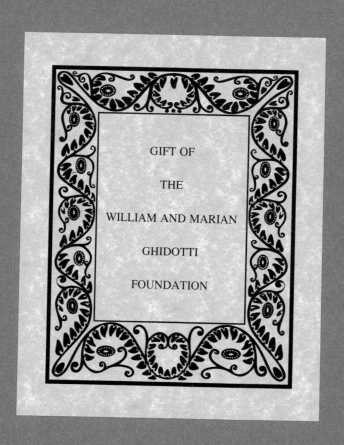

ELEPHANT WOMAN

ELEPHANT WOMAN

Cynthia Moss Explores the World of Elephants

LAURENCE PRINGLE

PHOTOGRAPHS BY
CYNTHIA MOSS

ATHENEUM BOOKS FOR YOUNG READERS

For Martha and Nan
—C.M.

Atheneum Books for Young Readers
An imprint of Simon & Schuster Children's Publishing Division
1230 Avenue of the Americas
New York, New York 10020

The text of this book is set in Italian Garamond

First Edition

Printed in Singapore

10   9   8   7   6   5   4   3   2   1

Library of Congress Cataloging-in-Publication Data:
Pringle, Laurence P.
Elephant woman: Cynthia Moss explores the world of elephants/
Laurence Pringle; photographs by Cynthia Moss.—1st ed.
p. cm.
Includes bibliographical references (p.) and index.
Summary: A biography of Cynthia Moss, world-renowned elephant researcher
in Kenya's Amboseli National Park, illustrated with her own photographs.
ISBN 0-689-80142-4
1. African Elephant—Kenya—Amboseli National Park—Behavior—Juvenile literature.
[1. Moss, Cynthia. 2. Zoologists. 3. African elephant. 4. Elephants. 5. Women—Biography.]
I. Moss, Cynthia, ill. II. Title.
QL737.P98P74   1997
599.67'4—dc21
96-40241
CIP   AC

CONTENTS

Mount Kilimanjaro looms over Amboseli National Park, where Cynthia Moss has come to know hundreds of African elephants.

ONE

Becoming Elephant Woman

Cynthia Moss often sits in the midst of a dozen wild African elephants. She knows each one of more than nine hundred elephants by sight. She knows them as individuals. She knows them as members of elephant families.

As the elephants move freely near her she observes their behavior—feeding, playing, resting. She treasures these times with elephants she has known for many years. She feels her research is "like reading a very good book about a family saga. You get so involved you don't want to put it down but you also don't want it to end."

Cynthia Moss's own life story is also quite a saga. Today she is one of the world's leading elephant researchers, yet she was not trained as a scientist. She is often asked about the roots of her unusual career. She has thought carefully about all of the people and experiences that influenced her life."They include my parents, of course, but also a special grandmother, horseback riding, some terrible losses, and serendipity."

Born in 1940, Cynthia was raised near the Hudson River in Ossining, New York. Her mother had been a legal secretary before

At age 7, Cynthia (left) and her sister, Carolyn, visited circus elephants.

resigning to raise Cynthia and her older sister, Carolyn. Her father was a publisher of several small-town newspapers and also ran a printing company. Both parents were avid readers.

For about half of each year, Grandmother Berthe Therese lived with the Moss family. Looking back, Cynthia believes that her French-born grandmother was a powerful model for her. "She was independent, capable, strong, and also adventurous," Cynthia recalls.

The family had pet dogs and cats, but it was horses, and riding them, that led Cynthia to appreciate and care about nature. When she was seven years old she began taking riding lessons. By age twelve she had her own horse, Kelly. Cynthia rode Kelly on trails through the woods. Being on a horse enabled her to get close to deer, foxes, and other wildlife. She began to feel that nature was something precious and wonderful. She remembers riding Kelly alone through the woods while a teenager as times of "total bliss."

Her love of riding led Cynthia to spend her junior and senior years of high school at a private boarding school in Virginia, where there was an excellent riding program. She graduated from Southern Seminary in 1958. With the help of an English teacher there she applied to Smith College in Massachusetts and was accepted.

Throughout her high-school years, Cynthia managed to be a good student despite some terrible losses. Her grandmother Berthe Therese died when she was fourteen. Her mother died of cancer when she was seventeen. Just a few years later, her father also died. Cynthia survived these heart-wrenching losses, and many years later realized that a lack of the usual family ties gave her a freedom to go out into the world that many others do not have.

At Smith College, Cynthia majored in philosophy and also took many courses in art and literature. "I wasn't particularly interested in science. And yet I was always interested in logic and careful reasoning, and was drawn to philosophy courses that called for rigorous analysis. Inside me was a scientist who wanted to get out and didn't know it!"

Graduating in 1962, Cynthia tried without success to find work in the making of documentary films. Hired by *Newsweek* magazine in 1964, she did research and reporting, including interviews, first on religious subjects and then on theater. It was exciting and fun for a young woman to live in New York City and work for a national news magazine. Cynthia might have stayed at *Newsweek* for many years if her feelings about nature hadn't been

Cynthia, 12, with her horse, Kelly, and sister, Carolyn.

reawakened. She became concerned about the destruction of wild habitats in the county where she had grown up and ridden horses. She joined the Sierra Club, which emphasizes the preservation of wilderness.

Cynthia longed to experience some of the world's great wild places. She was especially drawn to Africa. A college friend, Penny Naylor, who was living in Africa, wrote long, wonderfully detailed letters to Cynthia. In 1967, Cynthia took a leave of absence from *Newsweek* and set out on an extended visit to East Africa.

"Within a week, I had this overwhelming sense that I'd come home. I felt, this is where I belong, this is where my body belongs."

These feelings weren't sparked by African wildlife. "The wildlife," Cynthia says, "was the icing on the cake. It was the landscape, the light, the feel of the place that held me in some mysterious way."

Traveling with a friend, she visited Lake Manyara National Park in northern Tanzania. There she met Iain Douglas-Hamilton, a Scottish zoologist. In 1965 he had begun a pioneering study of elephant social life in the national park. To understand the social interactions of elephants he had to be able to recognize individuals by sight. He began to photograph every elephant he could find. There were over four hundred in the park.

When Iain Douglas-Hamilton drove toward elephants in his Land Rover to take pictures, they became alarmed and sometimes charged. There were many close calls, but he learned to approach the elephants more cautiously and they began to tolerate his presence. Furthermore, his photographs proved to be a reliable way to identify individual elephants.

Cynthia Moss explained why in her first book, *Portraits in the Wild*: "There was never any need to capture and mark elephants by putting brightly colored tags in their ears or painting numbers on them, as some other researchers had tried to do, because no two elephants are alike.

Like almost all elephants, Celeste has notches and other marks on her ears that can be used to identify her.

"An elephant's ears are not usually smooth along the outer edge but are almost always tattered in a unique way with U-shaped or V-shaped notches, holes or slits, or combinations of them all. The veins in the ears are prominent and also form unique patterns. Each elephant's ears are different and can be used for identification in much the same way as are human fingerprints."

Tusks are also an aid in identification. Cynthia wrote: "Some tusks converge, some cross over each other, some splay out, some curve upward, some are straight; also some elephants have only one tusk or a broken tusk, and a few have no tusks at all."

Iain Douglas-Hamilton had worked out the structure of elephant social life and was beginning to understand the family relationships when he invited Cynthia to join him on his daily observations. She had enjoyed watching wild elephants before, but now, "I stepped into the world of known elephants. Knowing something of the history of individual animals made them very three-dimensional."

Cynthia Moss's own history, her intelligence, and her skills of observing carefully and writing clearly about what she saw impressed Iain. He offered her a job as a research assistant. She took some time to decide, but finally accepted, feeling that "I had found something where whatever talents I might have had all came together."

She returned to New York in the fall to give up her apartment, job, and life in the United States. It was scary, starting a new life in Africa. But with the death of her parents, she had no ties to keep her in the U. S. Also, Cynthia says, "The scientist in me had leaped up and out. I realized how much I loved science."

Cynthia spent most of 1968 helping Iain Douglas-Hamilton study the elephants of Manyara. That fall, however, with his field work complete, Iain returned to England. Cynthia found no other work that would keep her in Africa, and she couldn't afford to stay without work. "This was one of the most unhappy times of my life," she recalls.

She wrote to all sorts of people and organizations in East Africa, seeking help or suggestions. Serendipity (unplanned good fortune) occurred. One of her letters was written to veterinarians Sue and Tony Harthoorn in Nairobi, Kenya, whom she had met through Iain. It arrived on the very day their assistant had suddenly left. Sue quickly invited Cynthia to join her for a while as a veterinary assistant.

"My goal was to one day do my own elephant study, but I had no background, no scientific credentials, except for my experience with Douglas-Hamilton." For the next few years Cynthia managed to stay in Africa and find opportunities to study wildlife. She assisted in research on zebras and other plains animals, and in a study of the feeding behavior of elephants in Tsavo National Park. She used her writing and editing skills, preparing a seventy-five-page background report for a film that was to be made about elephants. In 1971 she became the editor of *Wildlife News*, the newsletter of the African Wildlife Foundation. She also began to interview scientists who were studying wildlife behavior in Africa for her book *Portraits in the Wild*.

Finally, in 1972, David "Jonah" Western, an ecologist in Kenya, encouraged Cynthia to look into the possibility of studying the elephants of Amboseli National Park. A protected area of 150 square miles, Amboseli lies in southern Kenya, just north of Tanzania.

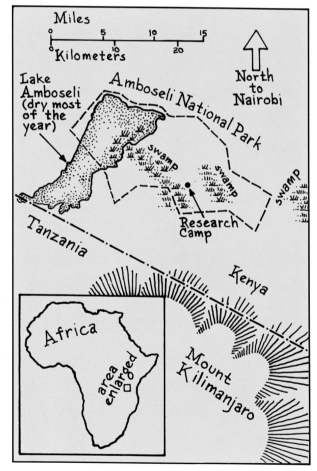

Snow and rain that fall on Mount Kilimanjaro provide water for swamps in and near Amboseli National Park. Elephants find food year-round in the swamps.

Early in her Amboseli studies, Cynthia used her own car as an off-road vehicle.

Cynthia discovered that the Amboseli population was ideal for study. All over Africa, elephants were being slaughtered for their ivory tusks and their range was being taken over by people. Elephant numbers were plummeting. Their family ties were unraveling. In Amboseli and its surroundings, however, the elephants had not been hunted much, nor had they lost range. The Maasai people who lived around Amboseli seldom hunted wildlife and took steps to keep out hunters, including illegal poachers. They also continued to allow elephants to roam on their land.

The lives of the Amboseli elephants seemed more free and natural than those of other elephants in Africa. Teamed with another researcher, Harvey Croze, in September 1972 Cynthia Moss began a formal study at Amboseli. It was part-time at first. Whenever she could leave her writing and editing work in Nairobi, Cynthia drove to Amboseli in her small Renault. Cynthia and Harvey began to identify individual elephants. Cynthia was delighted to be among Amboseli's elephants, but the future of the project was uncertain. She did not know that she had helped launch a unique long-term study. She never dreamed that elephants she met in 1972 would still be a vital part of her life twenty-five years later.

TWO

Meeting Elephant Families

The first step in elephant research at Amboseli National Park was to begin a "recognition file" of photographs. Whenever Cynthia or Harvey Croze located a group of elephants, they approached cautiously. They counted the elephants in the group and, using telephoto lenses, tried to get clear pictures of each animal's head and ears.

After returning to Nairobi, they developed the film and made prints of the best photographs. (They used black-and-white film; it is best for recording the fine details of elephant ears.) In her second book, *Elephant Memories*, Cynthia wrote: "I would take the photographs home and pore over them using a magnifying glass and with the aid of our notes try to sort out all the ears. It was immensely satisfying when a group started to take form and I was sure I knew who its members were."

Decades earlier, hunters in Africa sometimes wrote of shooting a bull elephant defending his "harem" of females. This myth had been erased by the research of Iain Douglas-Hamilton and others, so Cynthia and Harvey already knew that elephants live in family units that are made up of related adult females and their young. The

Each elephant family is led by its oldest and wisest female, the matriarch. This is the EB family, led by Echo.

juvenile offspring in a family range from newborns to calves up to ten years old. Each family is led by its oldest female, called the matriarch.

It is these wise old females, not bulls, who lead elephant families. Male calves usually leave their families between the ages of ten and fifteen. From then on the bulls live alone or in loose groups. Usually adult males join elephant families only when they are ready to mate.

In the early 1970s about six hundred elephants lived in Amboseli National Park. To keep track of all of these individuals, Cynthia and Harvey began giving them names. Eventually, finding names became a challenge. Cynthia has gone through several books that list hundreds of names to help parents choose a name for a baby. The very first family they photographed was called the AA family, with individuals given such names as Annabel, Amy, Alison, and Wart Ear. Wart Ear? Yes, she was also in the AA family. She had a distinctive wart on one ear and had been given that name before they assigned the family the AA code.

Some scientists believe it is best to assign numbers to individual animals being studied. Using names, they think, might cause researchers to associate their feelings about certain people with the animals. For example, a researcher who had a nasty neighbor named Bruce might let her feelings influence her observations of an elephant called Bruce.

Cynthia Moss says that no researcher at Amboseli has had this problem. "An elephant is so much its own being that it soon overshadows any association with a name. I, however, have the opposite problem now. When I am introduced to a person named Amy or Amelia or Alison, across my mind's eye flashes the head and ears of that elephant."

Members of the AA family drink water.

The leader of the TC family is Slit Ear (right), shown here with her three daughters.

Through 1974 the Amboseli research project advanced operating on a shoestring budget. Harvey Croze left for other work. Cynthia survived partly on her savings. She completed her book *Portraits in the Wild*, published in 1975. It received excellent reviews and also earned Cynthia some respect as a scientist.

In 1975 she received a research grant of $5,000 from the African Wildlife Foundation. Though this was hardly a large amount, it enabled her to begin devoting herself nearly full time to the study of Amboseli's elephants. She bought a tent and set up a camp in the park. She continued to use her own Renault, though it was far from an ideal off-road vehicle. In early 1976 Cynthia at last had a used Land Rover, a gift from the African Wildlife Foundation.

Living among the park's elephants changed Cynthia's research. She was able to gather information about their daily movements, relationships, and behavior. Each time an elephant group was sighted, she wrote down certain information: date, time, location, habitat type, activity of the elephants when first sighted, group size, family units present, and bulls present. Cynthia saw some elephant families several times a week and began to know them well.

"I would find one of the families I was concentrating on and spend several hours with it, either watching one individual for a given amount of time or observing the whole group and noting particular behavior."

Cynthia spent many hours watching family units called the TCs and the TDs. (They are the main subjects of her book *Elephant Memories: Thirteen Years in the Life of an Elephant Family*, which was published in 1988.) Slit Ear led the TCs, Teresia the TDs. "I became very fond of both Slit Ear and Teresia, Slit Ear because she had such a regal demeanor and Teresia because she was old and dignified and gentle and seemed very, very wise."

The year 1975, which marked the beginning of Cynthia's nearly full-time research, also marked the beginning of an awful drought in the Amboseli region. The lack of rain took a heavy toll on elephants, other wildlife, and on the Maasai people and their cattle. However, the drought helped Cynthia learn about elephant behavior in times of low rainfall, which are inevitable in East Africa.

Ordinarily, Amboseli receives only about a dozen inches of rain a year. It should be a desert with little life. South of the park, however, towers snowcapped Mount Kilimanjaro. Rain and melting snow on the mountain feed swamps and springs in the park. Even in the driest times, Amboseli provides wildlife with some lush green swampland.

Abundant rains and lush grasses are nature's signal for elephants to reproduce.

Rainfall in the park is vital too, though, and in 1975 the "short" rains that normally fall from late October to early December were disappointing. Then the "long" rains that normally occur from mid-March to early June also failed. These rains usually nourish grasses and other plants eaten by elephants and many other animals between June and November. Cynthia saw that the lack of food caused some elephant families to break up. Young mothers with new calves often left their families, perhaps to avoid competing with bigger females for scarce food.

Because of the scarcity of grasses and other plants, some of the mothers did not have enough milk for their new calves. Many calves died. Cynthia observed that "The stronger ones were able to survive for several months, but when they would normally begin feeding on vegetation to supplement their milk diet, at between three and four months old, there was almost nothing for them to eat.

"I was saddened but not surprised to find the first-year calves dying. What did surprise me was the disappearance of four-to-five-year-old calves." These calves stop suckling completely when their mothers have a new calf. When that milk supply ended, the calves had to find enough plant food in Amboseli's swamps to make up the difference, but many of them died. The cattle of the

Maasai people also died by the hundreds, and some Maasai began spearing rhinos and elephants, perhaps because they were competing with cattle for plant food.

Near the end of 1976 the "short" rains were abundant and the drought ended. Cynthia knew of seventy-eight elephants that had died. The drought had been a bleak, heart-wrenching time, but also an opportunity to see how elephants tried to survive. Cynthia noted that the T families had endured the drought with no deaths. Even their four new calves survived. Cynthia thought of several reasons for this but concluded, "More than anything I would guess that it was Teresia's knowledge which carried them through the drought."

Through the years, the wisdom of the older matriarchs has impressed Cynthia again and again. Elephants are highly intelligent, but a young one has much to learn. A newborn calf can soon stand and begin traveling with its family, but otherwise it is almost totally helpless. At first it doesn't know what to do with its trunk. It may trip over its trunk while walking. It also sucks on it in the same way a human infant sucks its thumb.

At first a calf kneels down and drinks water with its mouth. Several months pass before it learns to suck water into its trunk, then tip its head back and release the water into its mouth. Not until a calf is at least

Young calves may suffer during a drought because their mothers cannot produce enough milk.

15

This calf, shown learning how to use its trunk, will suckle milk from its mother for four or more years.

three months old does it manage to pluck some grass with its trunk and get it to its mouth.

In *Elephant Memories*, Cynthia wrote: "When they reached the stage of feeding in earnest, it was interesting to watch them learning what to eat and how to handle it. A calf will frequently reach up into the mouth of its mother or older brother or sister and pull out a bit of what they are eating. I assumed that in this way the calf was learning what species of vegetation to eat."

Although elephants eat mostly grass, they also consume a variety of trees, bushes, herbs, reeds, flowers, fruits, roots, and bark. They learn to avoid many other plants, some of which are poisonous.

From older elephants, calves learn how to deal with other wildlife, including hippos.

Again, there is much for a young elephant to learn. Besides learning how to blow dust on itself (to help reflect the sun from its body and to dislodge ticks), and to avoid dangerous animals and places, a young elephant has to learn vital lessons in getting along with other elephants.

These lessons begin with its own family, but reach beyond it too. Elephants seem to be attracted to other elephants. Families meet, travel, and feed with other families. They communicate by their body movements, by scent, and by their rumbles and other sounds, including low-frequency sounds that people cannot hear that may carry as far as six miles. An old matriarch, forty years old or more, may recognize hundreds of other elephants.

Elephants may even recognize the remains of fallen comrades. Cynthia Moss says, "They pay no attention to the remains of other species, but always react to the body of a dead elephant. . . . When they come upon an

Tulip's calf had to learn how to clamber over a huge log in order to reach her mother.

Elephants carefully smell and touch the remains of dead elephants. Perhaps they recognize the individuals that died. PHOTO COURTESY OF MARTYN COLBECK.

elephant carcass they stop and become quiet yet tense in a different way from anything I have seen in other situations. . . . They approach cautiously and begin to touch the bones. . . . They run their trunk tips along the tusks and lower jaw and feel in all the crevices and hollows of the skull. I would guess they are trying to recognize the individual."

In 1984, alas, the elephants of Amboseli had many bones and skulls to investigate because drought struck again. Conditions were even worse than in 1976, and the death toll, from lack of food and from spearings, was greater. This time the T families suffered losses. For Cynthia the greatest loss was Teresia, speared to death by Maasai who took her tusks.

Cynthia had grown very attached to Teresia and felt sad when she died. Her only consolation was that Teresia had lived nearly as long as an elephant can. She was sixty-two years old. Her sixth and last set of

18

teeth were badly worn, and she had trouble getting enough food. She moved slowly and followed the lead of Slit Ear. Her last-born calf, a son called Tolstoy, maintained a close relationship with her to the end. Tolstoy left the family when Teresia died and today is a tall, handsome bull of twenty-five years. He looks remarkably like his mother.

Drought is inevitable in the life of an East African elephant, and the droughts at Amboseli have revealed important knowledge about elephants. For example, Cynthia learned that the poor living conditions during a drought caused the elephants to virtually stop reproducing. They resumed breeding when rain again turned Amboseli green.

Cynthia rejoices when rain is abundant and the families she knows so well can feast and play in tall grasses.

Tolstoy, Teresia's youngest son.

THREE

Learning About Elephant Social Life

Cynthia Moss does not camp alone among the elephants and other wild animals at Amboseli. She has a camp manager who also serves as a cook. Through the years she has also added research assistants to the Amboseli Elephant Research Project, which she directs. At times other scientists live at the camp or nearby while studying monkeys, baboons, or other wildlife.

The camp is not fancy. It has a central dining tent, individual tents for work and sleep, and a kitchen with a dirt floor. A freezer is fueled by kerosene, and bread is baked over an open fire. All of the tents have thatched roofs. There is an outdoor "choo" (the Kiswahili word for toilet) and a shower whose water is heated by firewood. One important feature of the camp, Cynthia feels, is the lack of a telephone or other means of being interrupted by the outside world. (In case of an emergency there is a telephone at a nearby tourist lodge.)

One visitor was astonished to learn that there is no rifle or other firearm in camp. Amboseli is home to a rich variety of wildlife, including hyenas, jackals, wild dogs, zebras, giraffes, thirteen species of antelope, and some animals that might be considered dangerous to people:

The elephant research camp is set among palm trees in the south central part of Amboseli National Park.

rhinos, hippos, buffaloes, and lions. A black mamba, one of the most venomous of all snakes, may slither through camp in the daytime.

You simply have to stay alert when outdoors, Cynthia says. She feels safe in her tent. In 1981 a leopard ripped the screen window next to her bed, but the leopard was after her pet cat, Moshi. (A gray male, Moshi's name means "smoke" in Kiswahili.) Soon afterwards, Moshi was sent to live in Nairobi.

Although elephants are big enough and strong enough to crush humans or gore them with their tusks, they are rarely a problem. In 1978 a female named Tuskless led other elephants on a raid of the camp's food. The kitchen was wrecked. No one had been there to defend the camp. Usually, loud shouts will drive elephants away.

Elephants sometimes visit the camp. This is Tuo, the son of Tuskless.

In 1976 Cynthia photographed a large bull and called him M126. The next year, however, M126 charged and chased Cynthia in her Land Rover. She discovered that he had deliberately followed her for nearly a half mile. "I found this behavior totally strange, surprising, and not a little creepy. From that moment on I thought of him as 'The Bad Bull' and that became his name."

After some other close calls with Bad Bull, Cynthia made a rule for herself and other researchers: always have a clear escape route when near this elephant. In recent years she thought he might have mellowed, but she had another scary encounter with Bad Bull in 1995. Driving through a palm forest at dusk, Cynthia and filmmaker Martyn Colbeck were ambushed by Bad Bull. They made a narrow escape.

Bad Bull's behavior was unusual. Bull elephants are usually easy-going. Cynthia has concentrated her research on elephant families, but a colleague and friend, Joyce Poole, has observed Amboseli's bulls for many years. Joyce set about completing the identification photographs of bulls in 1976, while she was still a college student. By the time she graduated in 1979 (before beginning work toward a doctorate degree), Joyce and Cynthia had discovered some important information about African bull elephants. For about a three month period each year, older bulls go into *musth*—a condition that signals they are pursuing females and prepared to fight with other males.

This great old bull, Dionysus, probably broke a tusk in battle with another bull while in musth.

Musth had been well-known in Asian elephants, but the knowledge was based on captive animals. In wild African elephants, a bull first comes into musth when he is in his late twenties. By age forty a bull enters musth on a regular basis every year. Fluid flows continually from his temporal glands, which are located about halfway between an elephant's eyes and ears. The bull also dribbles urine, gives off a strong odor, and becomes aggressive. He even sounds a distinctive rumble. It turned out that Bad Bull was only "bad" when he was in musth.

A bull in musth leaves other males and searches for females that are in *estrous,* ready to mate. Bulls that are not in musth can mate with such females too, but usually give way to a bigger, stronger, and more aggressive musth bull. The females seem to prefer mating with a musth bull. They even give a special rumbling greeting call to him.

Among elephants, mating is a family event. When it occurs, usually all of the family members mill about in what Cynthia calls "mating pandemonium." They flap their ears and give an outburst of calls: trumpeting, rumbling, roaring, and bellowing. It seems like a celebration of the new life to come, but probably has more to do with attracting the biggest and best males.

A calf is precious to its mother and family, partly because elephants reproduce slowly. A human baby develops for nine months within its mother; an elephant calf does so for twenty-two months. So, just as an elephant family celebrates mating, it rejoices when a calf is born.

When a female is about to give birth, her family mills about, calling excitedly. This makes it difficult to see the actual birth. Also, many births occur at night. Cynthia Moss has seen only a few calves being born. In 1994 she was determined to witness this event because the elephant about to give birth was Echo, leader of the EB family, which Cynthia had observed since 1973. Through the years Cynthia had grown fond of Echo, an exceptionally gentle and wise matriarch. Echo and her family are the subject of Cynthia's books *Echo of the Elephants:*

The Story of an Elephant Family and *Little Big Ears*. Along with film-maker Martyn Colbeck, Cynthia has also made two public television films that cover a span of six years in the life of Echo and her family.

In 1994 Echo was almost fifty years old. She had produced at least eight calves in her lifetime. By early May she looked huge and seemed ready to give birth. Using special night vision equipment, Cynthia and Martyn waited for eighteen nights for the birth of Echo's new calf. When the moment came, however, Echo's family converged and milled about, "just as excited as I was," Cynthia said. "The family seemed almost delirious with excitement, perhaps because the matriarch had given birth."

After a few moments Cynthia was able to see the new calf through a forest of elephant legs. She watched Echo gently use a foot

As fluid flows from their temporal glands (between eyes and ears), elephants celebrate the birth of a calf, not yet on its feet.

In her care for Ely, Echo was helped by another daughter, Enid (right).

and her trunk to help her calf to its feet. "The tenderness expressed through the foot of an animal weighing three tons is truly wonderful," Cynthia says. She named the new female calf Ebony.

Wise old Echo knew how to take good care of Ebony. For example, a few days later she tested the footing of a swamp before letting Ebony step into it with the rest of the family. Being a good mother is another thing that a young elephant has to learn. In 1980 Cynthia had a heart-wrenching experience when she watched a young elephant deal with its first calf.

The mother was Tallulah, a seventeen-year-old member of Teresia's family. She was accompanied by Tara, a younger member of Slit Ear's family. Cynthia arrived in the morning, after the birth. She watched with growing concern as the calf made sucking sounds but failed to find its mother's nipples (between the mother's front legs). An experienced mother elephant stands in a way that enables her calf to begin suckling. Tallulah and Tara were no help at all. Three hours after its birth the calf had not fed and was lying down in the hot midday sun.

Perhaps to give the calf some shade, both elephants began to kick grass and dirt over it. In a few minutes it was almost completely buried. Cynthia noticed that the calf was breathing oddly. "I began to give up hope," she wrote in *Elephant Memories*, "and assumed I was watching the death of a newborn calf caused by the inexperience of its mother. I wanted desperately to do 'something' but knew I could not and would not interfere. My palms were sweating, my stomach was in a tight knot, and I wanted to shout at Tallulah to tell her what to do, but, of course, it would not have done any good."

Then, when the calf was four hours old, Tallulah used the tip of her foot to help it stand again. A few minutes later the calf finally

For several tense hours, Cynthia feared that Tallulah's calf would not survive, but there was nothing she could do.

By helping care for calves, young females prepare for the time they too will be mothers.

found its mother's nipple and suckled for more than a minute. Cynthia felt like cheering. By the next day the calf was suckling well and looking strong.

Watching an elephant mother and a whole elephant family take care of a calf reveals how much they value their young. It also reveals the workings of relationships and close bonds among members of the family.

Among humans, many girls love to take care of babies, perhaps because they feel that someday they will be mothers themselves. Among elephants, young females also play the role of mothers. Cynthia calls them babysitters or allomothers. In an interview published in the March–April 1993 issue of *Wildlife Conservation*, Cynthia said, "Allomothering is typical behavior of female calves between the ages of three and twelve." In contrast, male calves in this age range show no interest in younger calves.

The allomothers "are very attracted to small calves in or outside the family, and will spend quite a bit of time taking care of them. This relieves the mother of time-consuming calf-caring, so she can rest and get enough food. . . . Also, it's a learning experience for them, so when they have a calf they will know what to do. Families that have many allomothers in that age range have a much higher survival rate than families that only have males in that age range."

In Echo's family there was a good example of allomothering at work. Echo had given birth to Ely, who was crippled for a time and could barely walk (he later recovered). His older sister, Enid (then ten years old), would not leave him and helped Echo care for him. That strong bond between Enid and Ely remained until well past the age that calves are usually watched over. Even when Ely was five years old, Enid followed him around, stood over him when he was sleeping, and went after him if he wandered off and brought him back. If he cried out in a distress call, it was always Enid who went to his aid. Today, at nearly seven years old, Ely is more independent, getting ready to be on his own at twelve to fourteen years of age, but Enid is still often feeding or moving close to him.

Cynthia has witnessed many instances of the caring and close bonds in elephant families. In 1994, for example, Echo's mischievous new calf Ebony wandered off and was kidnapped by the V family, a large and aggressive group. They surrounded Ebony and didn't let Echo get to her daughter. Then Ella and the rest of Echo's family arrived. They formed a tight formation and charged into the V elephants, rescuing Ebony.

The close bonds in an elephant family are also shown when its members play, frolic in water, or wallow in

Calves play with other calves, and also with older elephants.

29

mud. Mud has its practical uses: it helps cool an elephant's body and offers protection from the sun. It is also fun to play in. In a mud wallow, Cynthia says, "there is often a great heap of calves all wiggling and scrabbling and slipping and sliding."

Calves play by climbing on top of each other, butting heads, trunk-wrestling, and chasing. Adult elephants too are sometimes in a playful mood. When good rains have produced a lush growth of grasses, elephants may get silly. They chase. They throw plants or spray water at each other.

Once, in 1980, Cynthia saw a spectacular show of two hundred elephants in

Elephant calves at play—mud wallowing and trunk-wrestling.

30

Dust rises as elephants excitedly whirl about in a greeting ceremony.

a playful mood on a vast open space at Amboseli. They all began to run with their heads down, letting their ears and trunks hang loose and flop about. Cynthia calls this "floppy running." And as all two hundred elephants ran, they let out a wild chorus of trumpeting.

Of all elephant social interactions, the one that most affects Cynthia is the greeting ceremony, especially when closely bonded elephants are reunited after being separated. The elephants click their tusks together and intertwine their trunks. They flap their ears in greeting. All members of the family do this while whirling about. Fluid streams from their temporal glands like tears. And the air is full of elephant rumbles and trumpets.

After more than twenty years of watching elephants, Cynthia Moss still feels a tremendous thrill at witnessing a greeting ceremony. In *Elephant Memories* she wrote, "Somehow it epitomizes what makes elephants so special and interesting. I have no doubt even in my most scientifically rigorous moments that the elephants are experiencing joy when they find each other again. It may not be similar to human joy or even comparable, but it is elephantine joy and it plays a very important part in their whole social system."

31

The oldest and wisest females lead their families in search of food.

FOUR

Working to
Save Wild Elephants

Elephants communicate by touch, body movements and positions, scents, and sounds. Their ears alone send important messages. When a matriarch flaps her ears in a sliding motion against her neck and shoulders, making a rasping sound, it means, "It is time to go. Follow me." Ears held in other positions send other messages, including threats.

People understand only a little of elephant communication. Elephant sounds alone are full of mystery. At least thirty different sounds have been detected. Parts of some calls are below the range of human hearing and may enable elephants to communicate as far away as six miles.

The mystery of elephant sounds is being investigated by Karen McComb of Sussex University. This is just one focus of the research underway at the Amboseli Elephant Research Project. Other researchers are trying to answer other questions. For example, by collecting DNA samples from bull elephants they can begin to understand how all of Amboseli's elephants are related genetically. Also, in 1996, Iain Douglas-Hamilton began to work again with Cynthia, this time to attach radio collars to elephants. Signals beamed from a satellite to the radio collar give the exact location of the elephants. The data about the elephants' travels, day and night, are recorded in the collars themselves. This information can be picked up by another radio and stored in a computer.

As director of research, Cynthia spends considerable time in Nairobi and has less time than before to observe the ongoing sagas of elephant families. She has, however, used special infrared lights to observe Echo and her family. She said, "Being with elephants at night is like entering the world of phantoms. On their huge spongy feet they move with barely a sound, and their ivory tusks almost glow in the dark."

She finally saw Echo's whole family lie down to sleep. In the daytime, calves lie down, but adults almost always rest while standing. In the night, she was able to see every elephant reclining in the grass. They slept deeply and even snored. Echo was the last to lie down and the first to rise. Some of these night scenes appeared in the second film for television about Echo's family that was made by Cynthia Moss and Martyn Colbeck. Cynthia and Martyn are now at work on a third film. She enjoys this work, partly because making documentary films was once her goal, but also because such films can influence people. In the late 1980s, Cynthia and other elephant conservationists decided that something had to be done to save Africa's elephants.

Filmmaker Martyn Colbeck (shown here with Ebony) and Cynthia Moss have made two films about Echo and her family.

The value of elephant ivory led hunters (mostly illegal poachers) to kill many thousands of elephants. A population of 1.3 million African elephants in 1979 plunged to about 600,000 in 1989. Poachers started with the big males because they have the biggest tusks. When they became scarce they began killing the older females, the matriarchs, and finally younger males and females and even calves. Eventually, Cynthia explains, "The entire social structure of the elephant family was destroyed, with just orphans and a few teenagers in some areas."

Some conservationists urged an international ban on trade in products made of ivory. At first Cynthia doubted whether a ban would work, but the slaughter of elephants was so relentless that she joined the effort to establish one. In 1990 an international treaty barred trade in elephant ivory. The demand for ivory and its price dropped, allowing elephant numbers to recover in some areas.

Cynthia does not enjoy the political work that is sometimes needed to help elephants. However, she has found ways to influence political leaders and others. In 1988 she and Joyce Poole traveled to Washington, D.C., where they urged the African Wildlife Foundation (AWF) to take steps to save African elephants. The AWF launched a

Biologists and conservationalists were appalled that thousands of Africa's elephants were being killed for their tusks.

When elephants range outside of parks, they may eat crops of people who farm nearby.

massive public awareness campaign. "The aim was to make people realize that elephants are highly intelligent, long-lived animals with a complex social structure. Each death has repercussions, and it was important that the public know that an elephant has to die in order for a consumer to have a piece of ivory jewelry."

Cynthia and Joyce agreed to put their research aside whenever there was an opportunity to tell people about elephants and their plight. Sometimes their observations of elephants were neglected for several days in a row while they gave tours and information to television reporters and magazine and newspaper journalists from all over the world. "One way or another," Cynthia said, "we were trying to show what elephants are, what we were going to lose." Cynthia's own work on the films about Echo's family and the book *Echo of the Elephants* were part of her effort.

Some day, Cynthia hopes, it will be considered unthinkable to kill an elephant. That day is a long way off. Even if poaching for ivory is totally halted, elephants may be killed because they eat farm crops. As the human population of Africa grows the wild habitat for elephants shrinks, and people and elephants clash. Elephants have always ranged beyond the borders of national parks. Now, increasingly, they find land being farmed right up to the parks' borders.

Luckily, there is only one area outside of Amboseli where there are farms, but the elephants have caused problems there. In the 1960s there were an estimated 1,200 elephants in the Amboseli area. Numbers decreased due to poaching and drought, but a long period of good rains and peaceful conditions has allowed elephant numbers to grow once again. More than nine hundred elephants now live in and near the park. Some of the areas where they used to roam have been taken over by farmers, and some elephants that raid farms have been killed.

Still, when the traditional Maasai people are asked if they want elephants killed or removed, many of them reply, "Oh, no. They have always been here." Cynthia shares these feelings about elephants being a vital part of the whole place. The Amboseli landscape without elephants would be like having Amboseli without Mount Kilimanjaro looming over it.

The elephant population of Amboseli remains one of the most undisturbed in all Africa, but trouble lurks for them just beyond the park's borders. This became tragically clear in 1994, when three of the park's oldest and best-known bulls crossed into Tanzania. Just a short distance

Sleepy was among the bulls shot by hunters when the elephants walked beyond park boundaries. PHOTO OF CARCASS COURTESY OF SOILA SAYIALEL.

across the border they were shot and killed by German and American sport hunters. The men had permits to hunt elephants in Tanzania.

Cynthia learned of the killings with horror and anger. The three bulls, including one named Sleepy, were among Amboseli's most important breeders. Also, as residents of the park the bulls were all quite tame and unafraid of people in vehicles. At least one was reportedly shot from or near a vehicle, a violation of Tanzanian hunting rules. In disgust, Cynthia said, "There is nothing sporting about shooting a relaxed and trusting Amboseli elephant. It would be like shooting a pet poodle."

She contacted the news media about this tragedy, and news reports echoed her outrage. The headline in *The London Times* read, *"Hunters" Kill Kenya's Tame Elephants*. A flood of criticism caused the Tanzanian government to temporarily ban hunting in the border region. Cynthia and others are trying to persuade the Tanzanian government that a tourism business in that area, luring people to see the elephants, would be more profitable in the long term than selling hunting permits. In neighboring Kenya, there is no sport hunting. Elephants, especially Amboseli's magnificent big bulls, are recognized as vital tourist attractions. They bring in many thousands of dollars each year, not just a one-time license fee.

Researchers at Amboseli include Kenyan women who observe elephants and share Cynthia's concern about them.

Wise and gentle, Echo cares for her latest calf, Ebony.

Cynthia continues to work with other researchers to save some of Africa's wild elephants. She has found the training of her three assistants, all young African women, to be particularly rewarding. Soila Sayialel, Norah Njiraini, and Katito Sayialel are as dedicated and passionate about the elephants as she is. Cynthia relies on them to keep up the elephant monitoring while she is pursuing other aspects of the project in Nairobi and abroad, and feels confident that the elephants are in good hands and will be for many years to come.

Cynthia still treasures the time she can spend in Amboseli, watching elephants. Although she is now well-respected as a scientist, she lacks the science degrees that would allow her to get research funds from the National Science Foundation and similar sources. So she returns to the United States for several weeks each year, seeking research support from foundations and individual people who share her deep feelings for elephants.

The long-term studies at Amboseli have caused people all over the world to appreciate elephants and to take steps to save them. This may be the greatest value of the research. However, in 1995 an incident occurred that showed a small but still vital way that knowledge of Amboseli's elephant population can also be put to use.

In September, a Maasai herdsman found a two-to-three-month-old male calf stuck in a well west of the park. Its mother was missing. Kenya Wildlife Service rangers rescued the calf and managed to feed it a special soy-milk formula. The calf did not become an orphan, however, because Cynthia's assistants figured out who the calf's mother was and set out to find her. By knowing every individual in the population, they were able to pinpoint the likely mother, Qatara. When they found her, she was indeed missing her youngest calf! With considerable effort the calf was brought to her, and they were successfully reunited.

Cynthia hopes that this rescued calf, and Ebony, and many, many other African elephants are alive and well long after she is gone. Although she has had some regrets about not having had a family of her own, she is glad to devote all of her time and energy to elephants, especially to the Amboseli individuals and families she knows and admires so much. Cynthia says, "I'll stand by them for the rest of my life."

The Amboseli elephants have been lucky so far. Most of Africa's elephants are rapidly losing the land they have lived on for thousands of years. And poachers who hunt them for their ivory tusks are an ever-present danger. If you'd like to support Cynthia Moss's work and help the elephants remain safe, please send a donation to or request further information from:

Amboseli Elephant Research Project
African Wildlife Foundation
1717 Massachusetts Avenue, N.W.
Washington, D.C. 20036

Toll free: 1-888-4-WILDLIFE / www.awf.org

FURTHER READING

Holloway, Marguerite. "Profile: Cynthia Moss, On the Trail of Elephants." *Scientific American*, December 1994, pp. 48–50.

Moss, Cynthia. *Echo of the Elephants: The Story of an Elephant Family*. New York: William Morrow and Company, 1992.

———. *Elephant Memories: Thirteen Years in the Life of an Elephant Family*. New York: William Morrow and Company, 1988.

———. "Getting to Know a Population." Chapter 7 in *Studying Elephants*, a technical handbook of the African Wildlife Foundation, edited by Kadzo Kangwana. Nairobi, Kenya: African Wildlife Foundation, 1996.

———. *Little Big Ears: The Story of Ely*. New York: Simon & Schuster, 1997.

———. *Portraits in the Wild: Animal Behavior in East Africa*. Second Edition. Chicago, IL: University of Chicago Press, 1982.

Petersen, Karen. "Elephants I Know" (interview with Cynthia Moss). *Wildlife Conservation*, March–April 1993, pp. 38–43.

Poole, Joyce. *Coming of Age with Elephants: A Memoir*. New York: Hyperion, 1996.

INDEX